Sarafina
This is a First Edition Book.

Published in 2010 by

Zorilla Entertainment Ltd,

Oak Cottage Studios,

Leigh On Mendip,

Somerset,

BA3 5QP

Text Copyright © 2010 Zorilla Entertainment Ltd

Illustration Copyright © Zorilla Entertainment Ltd

The moral rights of the author and illustrators have been asserted.

Printed in the UK by
Butler, Tanner & Dennis

ISBN 978-1-907430-09-1

www.bushtales.com

For the Love of Victoria!

ILLUSTRATIONS BY
FABRIZIO PETROSSI

COLOURING BY
VALERIA TURATI

ORIGINAL OIL PAINTING BY
KIRSTEN HARRIS

SARAFINA

WRITTEN & CREATED BY
MATTHEW R JAMESON

Sarafina, Sarafina, Sarafina,

Sarafina was a beauty Queen.

She was a jewel of divine inspiration,

The most exquisite Cheetah was she.

Many a'cheetah came from afar,
In the hope to win Sarafina's heart,
But none seemed to flatter
her beauty and grace,
And one by one she turned them away.

Soon word of her vanity
spread through the plains,
And in time she found
no more cheetahs came.

Sarafina, Sarafina, Sarafina,
Sarafina lived all alone,
And soon she gave up any hope,
A King would share her throne.

And then one day a handsome Prince,
entered her domain.
Ukari's grace entranced her,
And set her heart aflame.

Enchanted by her beauty too,
His heart began to sing,
The Prince asked Sarafina,
If he could be her King.

'Now handsome is as handsome does,
But is he **worthy** of my love?
Would my Prince provide for me?
Would my Prince look after me?'

'This Prince must prove he loves his Queen,
A **worthy** prince must worship me!'

Sarafina told Ukari
she'd not eaten for a month.
Overcome by hunger,
she had no more strength to hunt.

Without a pause the Prince set forth,
a feast he caught his Queen.
'This Prince he does provide for me,
a **worthy** Prince indeed!'

Sarafina told Ukari
she had trampled on some thorns.
Overcome by pain,
she had to rest her aching paws.

By chance it was a special night,

the Baobab was to flower,

And Ukari knew its nectar had a magical, healing power.

Without a pause the Prince set forth
and to the tree he went.
He climbed into the branches
and picked a flower, lush with scent.

When the Prince returned,
her heart began to sing.
My Prince, she thought
*looks after me
and he should
be my* **King.**

But something happened unforeseen.....

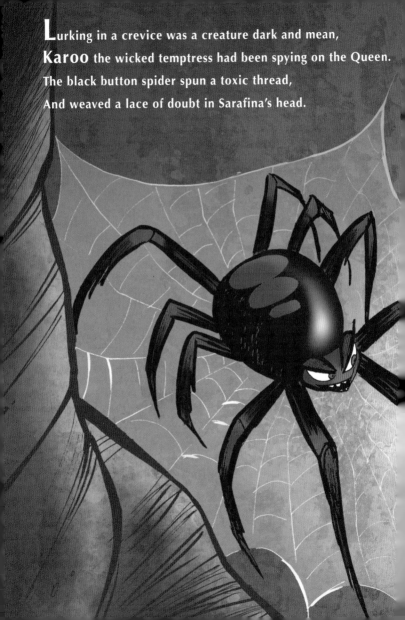

Lurking in a crevice was a creature dark and mean,
Karoo the wicked temptress had been spying on the Queen.
The black button spider spun a toxic thread,
And weaved a lace of doubt in Sarafina's head.

'A Prince is just a Prince,
if he simply shows his Queen,
He can muster up a feast
or pick flowers from a tree.
But a Prince becomes a **King**
if he can prove to you one thing,
He would sacrifice his being
and **die** for his Queen!'

Ukari was a'sleeping,
when he heard a chilling scream,
To the horror of the Prince
hyenas mobbed the frightened Queen.

Without a pause the Prince set forth
and **leapt** into the pack,
Sarafina took her chance
and escaped the fierce attack.

But Ukari's fate was stricken,
outnumbered ten to one,
A cloud of dust engulfed them
and cloaked the savage throng.

The cackling of hyenas
filled the air with ghastly cheer,
The pack emerged unharmed
but the Prince had disappeared.

Sarafina, Sarafina, Sarafina,
Sarafina what had she done!
For vanity ruled Sarafina's heart,
only loneliness she'd won.
Forty days and forty nights
she cried herself to sleep,
The tears that trickled down her face
forever stained her cheeks.

And every night,
by the light of the moon,
upon a star she yearned.
Begging for forgiveness,
and for her Prince to be returned.

Sarafina, Sarafina, Sarafina,
Sarafina was a tale of woe,
But wishes can come true,
hence there's one more truth to know.
One night across the moon lit plains,
as she wished upon a star,
Her sorrow seemed to drift away,
she forgot her heavy heart.

And then appeared a handsome Prince,
her heart was set aflame,
She knew his grace and majesty,
Ukari was his name.

No words need pass between them,
for their love was plain to see.
Sarafina and **Ukari**,
lived as **one**,
as **King** and **Queen**.